This   to:

....

Consultant: Barbara Taylor
Editor: Lauren Taylor
Designer: Elaine Wilkinson

First published in the UK in 2012 by
QED Publishing
A Quarto Group company
230 City Road
London EC1V 2TT

www.qed-publishing.co.uk

A catalogue record for this book is available from the British Library.

ISBN 978 1 84835 875 1

Printed in China

Owl's Winter Rescue

Anita Loughrey
and Daniel Howarth

QED Publishing

Owl sat watching over the wood.
Heavy snow had turned it into
a glittering wonderland.

"Winter is here," said Owl, and fluffed out her feathers.

"The days are getting darker and colder."

Owl spread her wings and
flew silently over the meadow.
She knew Mouse was sleeping
in her winter nest below.

The sun was
low in the sky,
giving the trees
long shadows.

"Look at all the
little prints
in the snow,"
said Owl.
"I wonder where
they go?"

Owl followed the
footprints to the pond.

Owl circled the pond.
Cobwebs shimmered in the
shrubs, and icicles sparkled
like diamonds.

At the edge of the
frozen pond, Rabbit was
sniffing at the ice.

It was so slippery that Rabbit
soon tumbled onto the ice.

Squirrel came scrambling up to the edge.
"I wouldn't be out on that ice
if I were you, Rabbit!" he said.

Rabbit tried to
hop away, but all
he could do was
slip and slide...

...and stumble all
over the ice.

"Be careful!" said Owl.

Suddenly, the ice started to crack.
Rabbit tried to stay still. The crack grew.
"Quick, run!" cried Owl.

The ice broke and Rabbit fell into
the freezing cold water. His front paws
scrabbled at the edge of the ice.

Owl swooped down
and lifted Rabbit out of the
water and into the air.

Rabbit's fur was wet
and he was shivering all over.
"You rescued me!"
said Rabbit.

Owl fluttered down to the
ground and put her wing around
Rabbit to keep him warm.

"Be careful where you step, Rabbit, or you'll get into trouble again," said Owl.

"Thank you for saving me, Owl," said Rabbit. "I'm so happy to be home!"

Winter activities

Fun and simple ideas for you and your child to explore together.

Build a cotton-wool snowman. It doesn't have to be snowing to make a snowman. Use cotton wool for his snowy head and body, pipe cleaners for his arms, and coloured paper for his hat, scarf and face. Use glue to secure the pieces onto a sheet of card. This would make a great greetings card!

Make paper snowflakes. Pretty paper snowflakes are a great way to decorate a bedroom in winter. Cut out circles of white paper or card, fold in half three times, then snip out small shapes from the paper with scissors. Unfold your beautiful creations and attach them to the window with sticky tack.

Create a wintery collage. Collect small sticks and cotton wool balls and glue them onto card to make a tree shape. You could use silver card to make your collage even more wintery and even make some mini paper snowflakes to add to the background.

Act out the story with your child. Use paper, pens, pencils and paints to make masks of Owl and her friends. Can your child remember anything the characters said? Does your child want to act out the story as it is in the book, or do they want to change the story in their own way?

What did we learn about winter?

❄ **Winter is a cold season in some parts of the world.** It is cold because the part of the Earth where it is winter is turned away from the Sun's warmth at this time of year. Many plants have a long rest over the winter, but survive as seeds or bulbs hidden underground.

❄ **Mouse is sleeping in her winter nest.** Animals spend a lot of time resting and sleeping in warm nests or burrows during the winter. A few animals go into such a deep sleep that they sleep right through the winter! This very deep sleep is called hibernation.

❄ **Owl fluffs out her feathers to keep warm.** Animals keep warm in winter by growing a thick fur coat or more feathers. Birds often fluff out their feathers in winter. This traps warm air from their body between their feathers, like a feather duvet.

❄ **It is snowing in the wood.** If the air temperature is very cold, tiny drops of water inside clouds freeze into ice crystals. These crystals join together to make six-sided snowflakes, which fall to the ground as snow.

❄ **Owl sees footprints in the snow.** It is easy to see and follow animal tracks in the snow. If the snow is very deep, however, it is hard for animals to move about. Animals may have to dig through the snow to find plants to eat.